To the memory of Amber Dextrose, Pod, Colin, Nuncle, Penny Dreadful,
and Math vab Mathonwy—best of cats, best of friends
—J.Y.

Text copyright © 2011 by Jane Yolen
Jacket art and interior illustrations copyright © 2011 by Jim LaMarche

All rights reserved. Published in the United States by Random House Children's Books,
a division of Random House, Inc., New York.

Random House and the colophon are registered trademarks of Random House, Inc.

Visit us on the Web! www.randomhouse.com/kids

Educators and librarians, for a variety of teaching tools, visit us at www.randomhouse.com/teachers

Library of Congress Cataloging-in-Publication Data
Yolen, Jane.
The day Tiger Rose said goodbye / Jane Yolen ; illustrations by Jim LaMarche. — 1st ed.
p. cm.
Summary: A cat whose kitten days are far behind her says goodbye to her human family, and the
animals and places that have made her life special, before leaving this life behind.
ISBN 978-0-375-86663-0 (trade) — ISBN 978-0-375-96663-7 (lib. bdg.)
[1. Cats—Fiction. 2. Death—Fiction. 3. Country life—Fiction.] I. LaMarche, Jim, ill. II. Title.
PZ7.Y78 Day 2011
[E]—dc22
2010013548

MANUFACTURED IN CHINA

10 9 8 7 6 5 4 3 2 1

First Edition

The Day Tiger Rose Said Goodbye

By Jane Yolen
Illustrated by Jim LaMarche

RANDOM HOUSE 🏠 NEW YORK

The day Tiger Rose said goodbye
was a soft spring day,
the sun only half risen.
Little brilliant butterflies,
like bits of colored paper,
floated among the flowers.

Tiger Rose had been born in the city,

but now she lived in the country

in a house filled with laughter and cat treats.

There, a boy and a girl loved her,

a dog named Rowf tolerated her,

and two grown-ups called Mom and Pop

let her sit on the sofa

as long as she did not use her claws.

But Tiger Rose was tired now

and she had gotten slow,

her kitten days so long ago

they were only small sparks of memory,

as fleeting as the butterflies.

Her back legs sometimes hurt

and she had a ringing in her ears.

She no longer had an appetite for chasing food.

Tiger Rose was getting ready to say goodbye.

High in the pine a solitary jay scolded,

"Do not come here, Tiger Rose.

Do not come here."

Rowf slept on the first step of the house,

nose on brindle paws.

"It is time," Tiger Rose said to the jay,

to the butterflies,

to Rowf, deep in a doggy dream.

She knew they did not listen to her

but she said it anyway.

It brought her comfort.

She meowed goodbye to Mom and Pop first

as they headed off in their cars,

though they barely noticed her.

She said farewell to the boy and girl

walking to school.

The girl stopped and gave Tiger Rose

a tickle under the chin,

as if she knew something was about to happen.

"Be easy," the girl whispered. "I'll remember."

Tiger Rose went to the bushes then

and said her goodbyes to them,

old friends, old shade.

Next she sniffed the green thrusts beneath the pine,

which smelled fresh and new, like kittens.

Tiger Rose touched noses with the moles and voles

and a chipmunk by the stone wall,

all of whom were surprised at her gentleness.

The little snake who lived behind the barn

startled and stopped slithering to look at her,

but did not speak except for a low hiss.

"It is time," Tiger Rose told him. "Goodbye."

She looked up at the nest of starlings under the eaves

and didn't even mind their squawkings.

"Goodbye," she whispered.

It sounded like a purr.

She stepped over anthills,

careful not to tread on any ants,

and walked slowly under an arch of azalea boughs.

With her tail, she saluted

the hive of bees behind the house

as they buzzed about their business.

Her purr was louder now.

At the feeders on the porch,

she said goodbye to a pair of buff-colored sparrows,

and to four goldfinches

who looked like a bit of flying sunlight.

"Goodbye. Goodbye."

At last, Tiger Rose sat down

to clean herself from head to tail.

When she was done, she stood and stretched,

making an arch of her striped back.

Clouds scudded across the sky,

flinging themselves

from one end of the blue to the other.

A stray wind puzzled through the trees.

The butterflies flitted from flower to flower

without speaking, without stopping

for longer than a moment or two.

Everything was either quick or dreaming,

but not Tiger Rose.

"It is time," Tiger Rose said again,

but now just to herself.

She lay down under the rosebushes,

heavy with early buds.

There she curled into a soft ball.

Closing her eyes, she envisioned

gathering for one last jump,

landing on a thin span of sun.

Then she walked slowly up and up and up,

past moles and voles,

chipmunks and snakes,

past the house,

where Rowf still drowsed,

past the blossoming azalea,

past the top of the pine,

past the scudding clouds,

and into the luminous blue sky.

She never once looked back

as she climbed away from life,

leaving her old and tired body behind.

Up and up and up she went,

and then she was gone,

now part of the earth, the air, the sky, the sun —

and all.